POKÉMON™

CATCH PIKACHU!

A DELUXE POKÉMON LOOK & LISTEN SET

BOOK • DVDs • HEADPHONES

Watch six episodes of Pokémon animation starring Pikachu, using the collectible
Pikachu headphones! Read about Pikachu in the 48-page book!

Catch Pikachu! A DELUXE Pokémon Look & Listen Set

Your Look & Listen Set comes with two DVDs of six action-packed TV episodes and specially designed headphones, all customized to your DELUXE Pokémon Look & Listen Set!

Publisher: Heather Dalgleish

Publishing Manager: Amy Levenson

Writers: The Pokémon Company International Editing Staff and Lawrence Neves

Designer: Megan Sugiyama

Art Director: Eric Medalle

Cover Designer: Chris Franc

Product Development: Drew Barr

Headphone Sculpting: Martin Meunier

Production Management: Jennifer Marx

Merchandise Development Director: Phaedra Long

Merchandise Development Associate: Katherine Fang

Project Manager: Emily Luty

Editors: Michael G. Ryan, Hollie Beg, and Eoin Sanders (for Pokémon) and Ben Grossblatt (for becker&mayer!)

Managing Editor: Michael del Rosario (for becker&mayer!)

Special thanks to Kellyn Ballard, Wolfgang Baur, Donaven Brines, John Renard, Blaise Selby, and Toshifumi Yoshida

Published by
The Pokémon Company International
333 108th Avenue NE, Suite 1900
Bellevue, Washington 98004 U.S.A.

1st Floor Block 5, Thames Wharf Studios, Rainville Road
London W6 9HA United Kingdom

12 13 14 15 16 9 8 7 6 5 4 3 2 1

Produced by becker&mayer!
11120 NE 33rd Place, Suite 101
Bellevue, Washington 98004 U.S.A.
www.beckermayer.com

ISBN: 978-1-60438-171-9

12214

Printed in Hangzhou China, 8/12

Visit us on the Web at www.pokemon.com

POKéMON™

WELCOME TO THE WORLD OF POKÉMON!

In this book, you'll learn about the most famous Pokémon of all, the amazing Mouse Pokémon Pikachu!

WHAT ARE POKÉMON?

From deep, dark forests to fields of grass to busy cities and quiet towns, the fantastic creatures called Pokémon are everywhere! Hundreds of different species share the Pokémon world, and each has its own special qualities and powers. Many people train Pokémon to compete in battles against other Pokémon!

Some Pokémon evolve, or grow, into other Pokémon, and sometimes they can evolve more than once. If a Pokémon evolves, it becomes more powerful than it was before, often with new traits and skills. Ash's Pikachu *could* evolve into Raichu—and you'll find out why it chose not to when you read all about its adventures!

PIKA-WHO?

Pikachu is an Electric-type Pokémon, and many different Pikachu live in the Pokémon world. But only one can be called Ash's Pikachu, a very special Pokémon that has traveled with its human Trainer across many different regions. In fact, Pikachu doesn't travel in a Poké Ball, like most Pokémon—it travels side-by-side with Ash!

So, what's a Pokémon type? Who's Ash? What's a Trainer or a Poké Ball? Now that you've entered the Pokémon world, you're about to find out!

POKÉMON TYPES

Every Pokémon has a type, which helps define what moves it can learn and how it matches up against other Pokémon in battle. Some, like Pikachu, are Electric types. These Pokémon are especially effective when battling against Water-type or Flying-type Pokémon, but they need to watch out for Ground-type Pokémon!

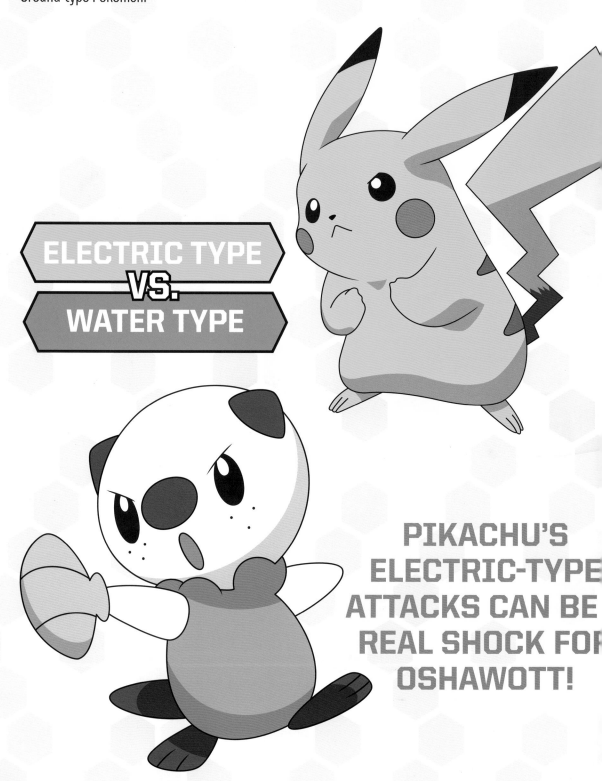

ELECTRIC TYPE
VS.
WATER TYPE

PIKACHU'S ELECTRIC-TYPE ATTACKS CAN BE REAL SHOCK FOR OSHAWOTT!

THE 17 TYPES

BUG

DARK

DRAGON

ELECTRIC

FIGHTING

FIRE

FLYING

GHOST

GRASS

GROUND

ICE

NORMAL

POISON

PSYCHIC

ROCK

STEEL

WATER

Dual-type Pokémon

Some Pokémon can even be two types at once, like Leavanny, which is a Bug- and Grass-type Pokémon. And when some Pokémon evolve, their Evolutions change types: for example, when Tepig (a Fire type) evolves into Pignite (a Fire and Fighting type).

LEAVANNY

WHAT ARE POKÉMON TRAINERS?

In the Pokémon world, people live, work, and play alongside Pokémon. Pokémon Trainers are people who want to make a life's work out of training, befriending, and competing with their Pokémon in Pokémon battles. Great Trainers try their hardest to understand and communicate with their Pokémon through love and friendship.

CATCHING UP WITH ASH KETCHUM!

Ash Ketchum is on a quest to become a Pokémon Master. His journey has taken him across many different regions and has included lots of adventures! With Pikachu by his side, he continues to face some amazing challenges as he gets closer and closer to his goal of being the best Trainer around!

Pikachu has been with Ash since the very beginning of his adventures. And though it doesn't like traveling in a Poké Ball, Pikachu is always happy to be by Ash's side. Together they form a partnership like no other in the world of Pokémon!

Ash is holding a Poké Ball, a special tool used by Pokémon Trainers to catch and keep Pokémon. But not all Poké Balls are the same—some of them are useful for catching specific Pokémon or are valuable for their increased success rate.

POKÉ BALLS

Poké Balls are absolutely essential gear for Pokémon Trainers who want to catch and train Pokémon. The Poké Ball is an electronic storage chamber for Pokémon. When Ash wants to catch a Pokémon, he throws a Poké Ball. When it opens, it captures the Pokémon and stores it until released. That's how Ash caught *most* of his Pokémon—but you'll soon find out that he and Pikachu did *not* meet this way!

There are many types of Poké Balls, and each has a unique purpose and strength. Here are some of them!

A Pokémon Trainer will usually receive several of these at the start of his or her adventure. These standard Poké Balls are good for catching the Pokémon a Trainer first meets, but serious Trainers will know all about the other Poké Balls they might come across.

DIVE BALL
Works especially well on Pokémon that live underwater.

MASTER BALL
Will catch any wild Pokémon without fail.

NET BALL
Effective in catching Bug- and Water-type Pokémon.

GREAT BALL
Has a higher rate of success in catching Pokémon than the standard Poké Ball.

DUSK BALL
Works much better at night or in gloomy places, like caves.

LUXURY BALL
Causes Pokémon caught in it to become more attached to their owners.

ULTRA BALL
Has even higher rates of success than the Great Ball.

HEAL BALL
Completely heals the wild Pokémon that it catches, which is great when a Trainer has worn down a Pokémon during an encounter.

REPEAT BALL
Effective for capturing Pokémon that have been caught before.

ASH, AND YOU SHALL RECEIVE...

Every great adventure begins somewhere, and Ash and Pikachu's adventure starts in Pallet Town in the Kanto region. But their adventure might never have happened at all had things actually gone according to plan!

After oversleeping the morning he is supposed to receive his first Pokémon from the famous Professor Oak, Ash turns up at Professor Oak's laboratory too late to get the Pokémon he wants—and the only one left is a Pikachu!

This isn't just any Pikachu, though. This one has an attitude, and it doesn't take long for it to show everyone just how defiant it can be, shocking Ash first, then Professor Oak, and finally shocking an enthusiastic crowd!

PROFESSOR OAK

As a novice Trainer, Ash has no idea how to handle a problem Pokémon, and Pikachu quickly figures that out. Even worse, Pikachu flatly refuses to get back in its Poké Ball, and Ash's clumsy attempts to control it don't help—at first, he tries to pull Pikachu along on a leash! Not the smoothest start for what will become one of the greatest Trainer and Pokémon friendships in the whole Pokémon world!

FLEEING FRIED FOE FUN

Ash and Pikachu encounter many foes on their adventures, but three of the most fiendish—and occasionally the most foolish—cause them trouble almost from the beginning. Jessie, James, and Meowth, a unique talking Pokémon, all work for Team Rocket, an organized crime group dedicated to stealing Pokémon—and their primary target is Pikachu! It all started in Viridian City...

Soon after he and Pikachu set out from Pallet Town, Ash manages to anger a flock of wild Spearow, and they attack Pikachu! Ash puts himself in danger to protect Pikachu, finally proving to his stubborn Pokémon that he can be trusted, and a fantastic friendship begins to blossom. On the advice of his new friend Misty, Ash hurries to Viridian City so Pikachu can be healed in the Pokémon Center. But before Pikachu can recover, Team Rocket attacks in an attempt to steal all the Pokémon inside the Pokémon Center!

In all the chaos, disaster seems certain—but then Ash's Pikachu manages to revive itself. Together with other Pikachu, it uses a powerful ThunderShock to hit Team Rocket, causing an enormous explosion, destroying the Pokémon Center, and stopping Team Rocket in its tracks!

TEAM ROCKET

Retreating to its Meowth-shaped balloon, Team Rocket escapes, vowing to return and steal Pikachu as a gift for their boss. It's a promise they constantly try to keep but always fail to deliver!

KANTO WAIT TO GO!

Now that Ash has won Pikachu's friendship, their journey through the Kanto region can really get going. Along the way, they battle incredible foes, see amazing sights, collect precious Gym badges, and eventually earn the right to compete in Kanto's famous Indigo League!

IT STARTS WITH A SHOCK!

The dust has hardly settled from the first encounter with Team Rocket before Pikachu is badly outmatched trying to help Ash in his first Gym battle in Pewter City. But that's not going to stop the plucky Pokémon! In the rematch against Gym Leader Brock, a combination of bravery, study, and compassion helps win Ash his first Gym badge.

SHOCKING FACTS!

Pikachu, Ash, their friends, and Team Rocket take a cruise on the same boat, but disaster strikes. The Pokémon are separated from their Trainers and shipwrecked on an unknown island—an island full of enormous robotic Pokémon! Pikachu and the others must work together with Team Rocket's Pokémon to reunite with their Trainers and escape from this dangerous place.

ELECTRIC SHOCK SHOWDOWN

Reaching Vermilion City after being lost for two weeks, Ash is entirely focused on finding the Gym. It's time to battle Lt. Surge and his Raichu, the evolved form of Pikachu. In the first round, Ash is quickly defeated and must rush Pikachu to the Pokémon Center to be tended by Nurse Joy.

Ash asks if Pikachu wants to use the Thunderstone they got from Nurse Joy to evolve into Raichu. It's a tense moment: though the two of them have learned to trust each other, their journey as Trainer and Pokémon is still just getting started, and if Ash pushes Pikachu to evolve when it's not ready, their friendship might suffer.

In the end, Pikachu decides not to evolve—it wants to stay as Pikachu and win just the way it is, and Ash respects that decision. When they challenge Lt. Surge's Raichu again, Pikachu proves that Evolution isn't everything, defeating Raichu with its superior speed and winning the Thunder Badge for Ash!

THUNDERSTONE

This special stone can help some Electric-type Pokémon evolve—including Pikachu evolving into Raichu, and Eelektrik into Eelektross. It's powerful enough that simply touching it can cause a Pokémon to evolve!

TOGETHER FOREVER!

After choosing not to evolve, Ash's Pikachu faces another big decision when the traveling companions discover a group of wild Pikachu living deep in the forest.

In the middle of the night, Team Rocket captures all the wild Pikachu in an electricity-absorbing net. Planning to take the entire clan of Pikachu back to their boss, they take to the sky in their hot air balloon, lifting off with the net full of Pikachu. Ash's Pikachu comes to the rescue by chewing through the netting, allowing all the wild Pikachu to escape. The menace of Team Rocket is blasted into the sky when Pikachu finally takes a chunk out of the hot air balloon!

After the rescue, it's clear that Ash's Pikachu is making friends with the wild Pikachu, and Ash decides that his Pikachu would be happier with its own kind. He starts to walk away, determined to leave Pikachu behind for its own good—but Pikachu is equally determined not to be left! It tracks Ash down, and as its wild friends cheer, Pikachu leaps happily into Ash's arms. In their hearts, they know they're a team for life!

PROTECTING PIKACHU

Not long afterward, this amazing bond between Pikachu and Ash is demonstrated again when Ash gives up his chance to win the Volcano Badge at the Cinnabar Gym—something he desperately wants—because he cannot bear to see Pikachu badly hurt by the Gym Leader's powerful Magmar. Of course, things work out fine in the end. But this time, Pikachu sits on the sidelines earning a well-deserved rest!

Ash and Pikachu have now been traveling Kanto for quite some time, but Ash needs Pikachu's best efforts to defeat Team Rocket at the Viridian Gym and secure the eighth Gym badge, the key to the biggest challenge yet—a shot at the Indigo League!

IT'S THE COMPETITION THAT COUNTS!

The journey to the Indigo League's opening ceremonies isn't easy for Ash and Pikachu—it's interrupted by shortcuts, showdowns, and more attempts by Team Rocket to ruin things for everyone.

Even with all these problems, Ash and Pikachu not only make it in time for the opening ceremonies, but they also manage to become torchbearers, carrying a symbol of inspiration for those competing in the League.

This definitely encourages both of them: they show great strength in battling their way through four tough rounds of League competition before coming up against more than they can handle when they face a competitor named Richie—and his own Pikachu!

They're disappointed at failing to win the Indigo League on the first attempt, but Ash and Pikachu have come a long way, finishing ahead of Ash's rival Gary Oak, winning the admiration of the people of Pallet Town, and proving themselves ready for whatever may come their way next!

ORANGE YOU GLAD YOU CAME?

Pikachu has some amazing adventures in the Orange Islands, just south of the Kanto region, but it isn't just a tropical vacation. From island to island, Ash and Pikachu battle for badges on their way to competing for the Orange League Trophy!

But they'll soon discover the Orange League isn't quite like other Leagues. There are only four badges to win here, and rather than typical Gym battles, a variety of tests awaits challengers to prove their worth.

TOIL AND TROUBLE

To help Ash win the Jade Star Badge from Luana on Kumquat Island, Pikachu participates in its first double battle! Ash chooses Charizard as Pikachu's battle partner, but the two of them don't get along at first—and before the real match begins, Pikachu and Charizard start fighting each other. Ash manages to calm them down and get them to cooperate, and the two battle their way to victory as strong allies!

NIGHT, NIGHT, DRAGONITE!

Even after battling and defeating the Pokémon Ditto when facing Drake, leader of the Orange Crew on Pummelo Island, Pikachu isn't done. To win the Orange League Trophy for Ash, Pikachu must return to battle and defeat Drake's powerful Dragonite. Though both Pokémon are near exhaustion at the end, Pikachu emerges victorious and is inducted into the Orange League Hall of Fame, along with Ash and the other Pokémon that competed in this exciting battle! Ash is thrilled with his victory and can't wait to get home to tell Brock all about it, and he and Pikachu get ready to head back to Pallet Town, where it all began.

SHOCKING FACTS!

While on Mandarin Island, Ash and Pikachu suffer a major loss to the famous Prima and her strong Pokémon Cloyster. Thanks to some advice from Prima, Ash decides that he wants his friendship with Pikachu to grow even stronger!

GOOD TIMES IN JOHTO!

Before they set off for the Johto region, Ash returns to Pallet Town for a battle with his hometown rival, Gary, and a visit to Professor Oak's laboratory. He decides to leave most of his Pokémon with Professor Oak—but of course he keeps his best buddy by his side! Pikachu is ready for more adventures, and as Ash and friends reach the Johto region, they find many new Pokémon and people to meet and places to explore.

RELENTLESS TEAM ROCKET

Even with all the new Pokémon to see in Johto, everywhere Pikachu goes, Team Rocket is sure to follow. Their desire to catch the Electric-type Pokémon doesn't weaken in the Johto region. Good thing Pikachu always has its friends along to rescue it so it can use an Electric-type attack to make Team Rocket blast off again!

PIKA-CHOOSE WISELY!

Why is Team Rocket's Meowth a very unusual Pokémon?
A) It's much bigger than Meowth are normally.
B) It can talk.
C) It is a different color from any other Meowth.

Answer: B) It can talk.

PIKACHU HELPS ASH WIN THE FIRST JOHTO GYM BADGE

Ash can always rely on Pikachu to be a great asset in his Pokémon team, and against Gym Leader Falkner and his Flying-type Pokémon, that's definitely true! Pikachu is a great choice against Falkner's Dodrio and Hoothoot. By using Thunderbolt, Quick Attack, and ultimately Thunder, Pikachu knocks out both Pokémon. Super effective!

LET'S CATCH IT, PIKACHU!

Pikachu and friends know that when they come to a new region, they're going to meet many exciting, never-seen-before Pokémon...and Johto doesn't disappoint! One cool Pokémon they meet is a Shiny Noctowl, and Pikachu is ready to help Ash catch this special Pokémon by using its Thunderbolt move!

GIVING THE WATER A LITTLE SHOCK

When Ash finds out about a Seaking Catching Competition in Johto, he wisely chooses his Pikachu to enter, since it has an advantage against Water types. Pikachu steals the show when it helps Ash catch a huge Seaking by hitting it with a well-timed Thunderbolt, and Ash ends up among the top competitors!

THE APPLE CORP!

When Ash and Pikachu find an apple orchard stripped bare, the owner Charmaine promptly decides that Pikachu is the apple thief! When Ash helps determine who's truly responsible, Pikachu meets a band of Pichu living in the orchard. They're guilty, but they're just so cute! When Team Rocket turns up, everyone works together to keep the villains from kidnapping Pikachu—and in the process, Charmaine and the Pichu make a pretty good team. They decide to keep working together to run the orchard.

TAKING TO THE SKIES!

On their way to Olivine City, Pikachu and friends come across a little snag—they need a plane to get there! They find one, but when they hit a big storm their plane starts to fall apart! With the help of their Pokémon friends, they manage to hold the plane together, but what will they do about the lightning? Pikachu to the rescue! It climbs on top of the plane and acts as a lightning rod, drawing all the lightning to itself!

A NEW FRIEND HATCHES

When Ash's Pokémon Egg hatches, out comes a Phanpy! The Team Rocket members try to steal it, but Pikachu is there to shock them with Thunderbolt. In the process, it accidentally gives Phanpy a little shock as well. So, Phanpy runs off, and it's up to Pikachu and the gang to go find it. Eventually, Pikachu and Ash are able to save Phanpy from being carried away by a raging river! It's a new start to a lasting friendship!

NOW YOU'RE PIKACHU, TOO!

Pikachu has always been Ash's most trusted Pokémon, but in Johto, his dedication to Pikachu grew when Ash was turned into a Pikachu by a magician! Luckily for Ash, it was only temporary, but he did get to see what it was like being a Pikachu like his good friend!

After Ash is eliminated from the Johto League Silver Conference, one of his fellow competitors, Harrison, tells him about the Hoenn region, where Ash can discover all kinds of new Pokémon. Ash and Pikachu decide it's time for new adventures in a new land—and once again, Pikachu is the only Pokémon Ash takes with him!

A TOUGH ROAD TO HOENN!

Right from the beginning of Ash and Pikachu's adventures in the Hoenn region, Pikachu isn't feeling very good: it's suffering from electric overload, which could be big trouble for the little Pokémon! Luckily for Pikachu this time, Team Rocket never stops trying to kidnap it—and Pikachu is able to discharge all that extra electricity right into Team Rocket's Pikachu-grabbing robot!

SHOCKING FACTS!

Unfortunately, Pikachu has a tendency to destroy its new friends' bicycles. Misty's bike got zapped shortly after Ash and Pikachu first met, and when they arrive in Hoenn, Pikachu manages to take out May's bike as well. But after the run-in with Team Rocket, she's just glad Pikachu is all right, and decides to join Ash and Pikachu on their journey through the region!

PIKACHU'S BIG MOVE: IRON TAIL

Pikachu begins to learn the move Iron Tail while in Rustboro City, mastering it just in time to defeat Rustboro Gym Leader Roxanne's Nosepass. The win earns Ash his first Hoenn Gym badge, the Stone Badge!

DYNAMITE DYNAMO BADGE

When Ash and Pikachu arrive in Mauville City so Ash can battle against Gym Leader Wattson for the Dynamo Badge, Pikachu suffers a familiar fate: electric overload due to high voltage exposure. This time, however, Pikachu uses all that extra energy to quickly defeat all three of Wattson's Pokémon—in fact, it only takes Pikachu one hit to knock out each of them!

A SCARE TO REMEMBER!

Team Rocket uses a robot to grab Pikachu— again!—but the robot falls into a sinkhole, flinging everyone far and wide. Meowth realizes that Pikachu has amnesia from the fall! Taking advantage of this, Meowth plants untrue memories in Pikachu's mind and then brings it over to Team Rocket, even though Meowth realizes along the way that Pikachu is very brave and kind. Fortunately, Ash is not far behind in tracking Pikachu to Team Rocket's base. When Pikachu doesn't remember him, Ash is heartbroken—but he isn't ready to give up so easily on his friend.

He hitches a ride on Team Rocket's hot air balloon, and when Pikachu tries to drive Ash away with a Thunderbolt, the balloon pops, and they fall together into a river! This fall restores Pikachu's memory, and the two best friends are united once more.

EPIC ALLIES, EPIC BATTLES

When Pikachu accidentally absorbs the mysterious Blue Orb, it makes the poor Pokémon lose control of its Electric-type attacks, but ultimately bonds it with the Legendary Groudon in an epic battle against another Legendary Pokémon, Kyogre.

IT'S RAINING BADGES

Pikachu saves the day again to help Ash win his eighth and final Hoenn League badge, the Rain Badge, in a battle against Sootopolis Gym Leader Juan. This is the victory that opens the way for Ash to enter the Hoenn League Championship in Ever Grande City!

YOU CAN'T WIN 'EM ALL...

For Ash and Pikachu, the Ever Grande Conference builds up to a battle between Ash and a Trainer named Tyson. They face off with their most loyal Pokémon, Ash's Pikachu versus Tyson's Meowth. It's Iron Tail against Iron Tail, and in the end, Pikachu just isn't tough enough! Tyson goes on to win the tournament!

PIKA-CHOOSE WISELY!

Which Ability does Pikachu have?
A) Static
B) Overgrow
C) Flame Body

Answer: A) Static

FINAL FRONTIER? NOT QUITE!

The Battle Frontier is a series of facilities across Kanto. The leaders, or Frontier Brains, of those facilities show hopeful challengers the front lines of Pokémon battles!

Pikachu plays a vital part in Ash's great success, helping him defeat all the Frontier Brains and collect their Frontier Symbols. But that's not all...

While here, Pikachu learns one of its key moves—Volt Tackle! This Electric-type move is extremely powerful and really comes in handy as Ash and Pikachu battle their opponents and fight off Team Rocket's continued attempts to steal Pikachu away!

Ash and Pikachu also learn from Gary Oak about the Sinnoh region, their next destination!

SIGNS OF SINNOH!

Pikachu explores mysterious Sinnoh, where the mountains and lakes are said to conceal a number of Legendary Pokémon. And when it comes to exploring new lands, Pikachu is not shy about jumping in and getting its feet wet!

STEALING HOME

Pikachu's adventures in Sinnoh start with a steal, as Pikachu falls (again) into the clutches of Team Rocket. However, Team Rocket is not known for keeping its act together, so in no time Pikachu escapes but is lost and alone. While Ash searches for his missing friend, Dawn is the key to getting Pikachu and Ash back together again.

Dawn wants to become a Pokémon Coordinator like her mom. Pikachu and Dawn's first meeting proves to be a disaster—for Dawn's bicycle! Pikachu accidentally destroys it with a Thunderbolt...but all is quickly forgiven, and Dawn decides to join Ash and Pikachu on their journey.

R IS FOR ROBOT

It's never over with Team Rocket, which gets back into the act with another attempt to steal Pikachu, this time with the help of a giant robot. It's up to Ash to bravely rescue his friend from Team Rocket's mechanical mayhem!

A NEW RIVALRY

As Pikachu and Ash explore the amazing Sinnoh region, they keep running into Paul and his tough Elekid. Paul is an arrogant Trainer who seems to favor harsh training methods. Battles with Paul are no piece of cake, that's for sure. The two Trainers first butt heads in a spectacular three-on-three battle that ends in a draw as Pikachu and Elekid are both unable to continue!

EVOLVING FRIENDSHIPS

Later, Paul's Elekid evolves into Electabuzz, and it and Pikachu get to know each other a little better — and even team up against the nefarious Team Galactic and a swarm of Golbat!

After Electabuzz evolves into Electivire, Pikachu is once more pitted against its fellow Electric type, as Paul and Ash battle in the Sinnoh League Championships. Pikachu gives its all and stands up for the team, and Ash goes on to win! The victory is bittersweet, as he and Pikachu bid farewell to their worthy rivals.

PIKA-CHOOSE WISELY!

Which of these is *not* one of Ash and Pikachu's primary rivals?
A) Paul
B) Gary
C) Brock

Answer: C) Brock

PIKA AND GOLIATH

A chance meeting in the forest with a super-hip Trainer, Sho, has Ash agreeing to fight but definitely not agreeing to Sho's repeated request that the winner keep the other Trainer's Pokémon. In fact, Sho has his eye on Pikachu because he wants to complete an Evolution chain (he already has a Pichu and a Raichu).

Pikachu considers Evolution again when it loses to Sho's Raichu and its Hyper Beam move, which Pikachu can't learn unless it evolves. The epic fight lands Pikachu at a Pokémon Center in critical condition, and even Team Rocket is worried!

Once it recovers, Pikachu again decides it's not interested in evolving but is determined to beat Raichu in its current form. After using some smart strategy from Ash, Pikachu is declared the winner!

A WHOLE NEW WORLD!

Ash and Pikachu set out to explore the Unova region together—and because it's very unusual to see a Pikachu in Unova, they're getting a lot of attention from the locals! With Pikachu's help, Ash is well on his way to the goal of entering the Unova League!

A SHOCKING WELCOME

Soon after arriving in Unova with Ash, Pikachu is struck by lightning from a mysterious thundercloud, and all of its Electric-type moves stop working! As a result, Ash's first battle with his newest rival, Trip, doesn't go so well. But don't worry—a second zap from another mysterious storm soon sets things right again!

THE BATTLE CLUB

The Pokémon Battle Club, first seen in the Unova region, is a place where Trainers and Pokémon can work out together and battle other Trainers. Ash meets a boy in the Accumula Town Battle Club who's very interested in battling Pikachu with his Dewott! Pikachu definitely has the advantage, until an emergency alarm cuts the battle short and they're forced to stop.

DANCING WITH THE DUCKLETT TRIO

A surprise sinkhole has Ash and Pikachu falling down a long tunnel that they soon realize is the work of Sandile, which has tracked them down so it can battle Pikachu. As the battle gets under way, there's more mischief going on: a trio of Ducklett steals Cilan's metal serving dome, Sandile's sunglasses, and Ash's hat!

When Ash catches up with the three Ducklett, he is surprised by their Scald and Ice Beam moves. The thieving trio then throws its loot at Ash to distract him and uses a pink umbrella to deflect Pikachu's Thunderbolt. Sandile and Pikachu's battle is effectively on hold until the Ducklett can be dealt with. And in doing so, Pikachu learns a brand-new attack: Electro Ball!

CASTELIA CITY GYM

When Ash challenges Burgh for the third Unova Gym badge, Ash sends Pikachu up against the tough Leavanny! Its String Shot leaves Pikachu wrapped up and off balance, and things look grim...but some quick thinking from Ash gets rid of the sticky threads, and Pikachu defeats Leavanny with a powerful Electro Ball!

THWARTING TEAM ROCKET...AGAIN

When Jessie, James, and Meowth steal all the Pokémon from the Nimbasa City Pokémon Center and make their getaway in a subway car, Pikachu thinks fast to get everyone out! Finding its friends in the pile of Poké Balls, Pikachu directs their attacks to help their car break away from the rest of the train. They escape just as Ash arrives, and then they all work together to send Team Rocket running!

NIMBASA CITY GYM

Pikachu is a key player when Ash challenges Gym Leader Elesa for his fourth badge, in Nimbasa City—though some persuasion is required for Ash to realize he can't win by himself!

MISTRALTON CITY GYM

Pikachu is a natural choice to help Ash battle Skyla, a Gym Leader who specializes in Flying types! After Ash's Tranquill gets worn out battling Skyla's Unfezant, Ash sends Pikachu in. When Unfezant swoops in with a hard-hitting Aerial Ace, Pikachu knocks it out of the sky with a perfectly timed Iron Tail and quickly follows it up with an Electro Ball for the win! Ash goes on to defeat Skyla and earn the Jet Badge—number six on his path to the Unova League!

SHOCKING FACTS!

Pikachu's friend Krokorok also battles in the Mistralton Gym. The two didn't always get along, though—when they first met, back when Ash's Krokorok was a wild Sandile, it grabbed Pikachu in its mouth and ran off!

SHINY GYM BADGES

Ash counts on Pikachu to help make his dream—of being a Pokémon Master one day—come true. And the route to becoming a Pokémon Master is long and filled with feisty Gym battles, eight for each region Ash has explored so far!

KANTO GYM BATTLES

 Boulder Badge from Brock in Pewter City

 Earth Badge from Team Rocket at the Viridian Gym

- Thunder Badge from Lt. Surge in Vermilion City
- Soul Badge from Koga in Fuchsia City
- Volcano Badge from Blaine at Cinnabar Island

- Cascade Badge from Misty in Cascade City
- Rainbow Badge from Erika in Celadon City
- Marsh Badge from Sabrina in Saffron City

JOHTO GYM BATTLES

 Zephyr Badge from Falkner in Violet City

 Rising Badge from Clair in Blackthorn City

- Plain Badge from Whitney in Goldenrod City
- Storm Badge from Chuck in Cianwood City
- Glacier Badge from Pryce in Mahogany Town

- Hive Badge from Bugsy in Azalea Town
- Fog Badge from Morty in Ecruteak City
- Mineral Badge from Jasmine in Olivine City

HOENN GYM BATTLES

 Stone Badge from Roxanne in Rustboro City

 Rain Badge from Juan in Sootopolis City

- Dynamo Badge from Wattson in Mauville City
- Balance Badge from Norman in Petalburg City
- Mind Badge from Tate and Liza in Mossdeep City

- Knuckle Badge from Brawly in Dewford Tow
- Heat Badge from Flannery in Lavaridge Tow
- Feather Badge from Winona in Fortree City

SINNOH GYM BATTLES

Coal Badge from Roark in Oreburgh City

 Forest Badge from Gardenia in Eterna City

 Cobble Badge from Maylene in Veilstone City

Fen Badge from Crasher Wake in Pastoria City

Relic Badge from Fantina in Hearthome City

 Mine Badge from Byron in Canalave City

 Icicle Badge from Candice in Snowpoint City

Beacon Badge from Volkner in Sunyshore City

UNOVA GYM BATTLES

Trio Badge from Chili, Cress, and Cilan in Striaton City

Basic Badge from Lenora in Nacrene City

Insect Badge from Burgh in Castelia City

Bolt Badge from Elesa in Nimbasa City

Quake Badge from Clay in Driftveil City

 Jet Badge from Skyla in Mistralton City

10 KEY PIKACHU BATTLES

All Pokémon love to battle, and Pikachu is one of the toughest battlers of them all! During its journey with Ash, Pikachu has won and lost many times, but it has never given up. Here are a few of Pikachu's most famous battles of all time—and some of the *little* battles that made a *big* difference.

1. KANTO: PIKACHU MEETS TEAM ROCKET

When Team Rocket tries to steal all the Pokémon from the Pokémon Center in Viridian City, Pikachu stops them! Though injured, Pikachu defeats Jessie and James with ThunderShock—the first time Pikachu beats the persistent criminals. Its explosive ThunderShock destroys the Pokémon Center—and impresses Jessie and James so much they swear to steal Pikachu for the Boss.

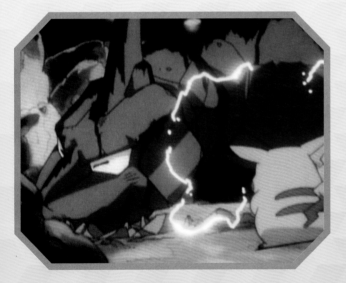

2. KANTO: A FRIEND IN PEWTER CITY

Battling is about both rivals and new friends. After Ash loses against Pewter City Gym Leader Brock, he and Pikachu work together to find another way to win. Pikachu uses its new Thunderbolt move and the Gym's sprinklers to defeat Brock's massive Onix. Brock and Ash become good friends soon after, and Brock joins Ash on his journey across the Pokémon world. It's a friendship that will last a lifetime!

3. KANTO: GARY OAK PACKS A PUNCH

Gary Oak is Ash's greatest rival in the early days, and he wins almost all their battles. After winning the Orange League, Ash feels more confident about a rematch, but things don't go as planned. Gary's Eevee is too clever, using tricky moves like Reflect, Double Team, and Take Down—and Pikachu is ultimately knocked out! The loss is humbling, but the two rivals learn that a League title is no guarantee of victory!

4. HOENN: PIKACHU'S NEW GROOVE

Pikachu hasn't always known how to use its signature move, Iron Tail. In fact, it learned how against Rustboro Gym Leader Roxanne. The Gym battle really puts Pikachu to the test when it is caught by Rock Tomb and blasted by Sandstorm. Fortunately, a Zap Cannon attack re-energizes Pikachu, and it lands its new Iron Tail for the win!

5. HOENN: THE BALLOON BATTLE

Pikachu learns another new move in a much crazier battle. Team Rocket tries to steal dozens of Pokémon Eggs...while flying in a balloon, using a giant mecha robot, and battling with Vileplume against Meowth and Munchlax. This epic battle teaches Pikachu the new move Volt Tackle, which will make all the difference in many of Pikachu's battles to come!

6. HOENN: A LEGENDARY CHILL IN THE AIR

When Ash wants to complete his Battle Frontier quest, he runs into Pyramid King Brandon and his Legendary Pokémon, the freezing Regice. Ice Beams and Thunderbolts crash through the arena, and Regice scores a direct hit, freezing Pikachu solid—but with an inspiring speech from Ash praising Pikachu's courage and persistence, the plucky little Pokémon manages to break free and defeat the Legendary Regice. And with Pikachu's victory, Ash enters the Hall of Fame!

7. SINNOH: EMPOLEON'S BATTLE PLAN

An epic three-round battle of two great Trainers pits Ash against Barry—and Pikachu isn't even Ash's first pick! Instead, Chimchar and Gliscor fight in the early rounds, but Barry's Pokémon are just too strong. It's up to Pikachu to earn a hard-fought victory over Barry's mighty Empoleon!

8. SINNOH: TWO POWERFUL OPPONENTS

This battle is big-big-BIG, as Ash and his team face off against Tobias, who uses Darkrai and Latios in the Sinnoh League Championship battle! Through sheer persistence, Pikachu knocks Latios down and out in the semi-finals! Though Tobias takes the Sinnoh League title, Ash lands his first final-four position at a top tournament—and Pikachu again manages to defeat a Legendary Pokémon!

9. UNOVA: A THIEVING TRIO

Three Ducklett steal a Sandile's sunglasses, Ash's hat, and Cilan's serving dome, and Pikachu battles to get them back! This isn't one of Pikachu's earth-shattering championship battles: instead, it's about helping out a new friend and stopping some rude bullies. Bonus: Pikachu learns a cool new move in this battle, Electro Ball!

10. UNOVA: PUT ME IN, COACH!

After a long journey across Unova, Ash squares off for a big battle with Gym Leader Elesa in Nimbasa City. At first, Ash tells Pikachu to sit out, but in the end, Pikachu convinces Ash to let it battle—though it takes a Thunderbolt to make Ash realize he needs Pikachu's help! Pikachu soon knocks out Elesa's Emolga and Tynamo and shows off its Electric-type style—all to help Ash win the Bolt Badge!

After facing so many opponents in their journeys together, Ash and Pikachu have become the perfect Trainer-Pokémon team. Whenever Ash is faced with a critical battle, he knows that he can count on Pikachu's loyalty and skills to save the day!

PIKACHU AT A GLANCE

Pikachu is Ash's first Pokémon and his best friend! It has traveled with him on all his journeys, ever since they first met in Professor Oak's laboratory.

Pikachu's big ears give it sharp hearing.

Pikachu's red cheek pouches can store electricity.

PIKACHU

TYPE: Electric
CATEGORY: Mouse Pokémon
HEIGHT: 1'04"/0.4 m
WEIGHT: 13.2 lbs./6.0 kg

Pikachu sometimes uses its tail to attract lightning bolts or other kinds of electricity.

Ash's Pikachu doesn't like being kept in its Poké Ball.

A TALE OF A TAIL

Pikachu discovered at the Castelia City Gym that its large tail is essential for its sense of balance, and when it can't move its tail, it has a hard time aiming its attacks. Pikachu can also use its Iron Tail move to smack down opponents.

IT'S ELECTRIC!

Pikachu attacks and defends with crackling electrical attacks. Wild Pikachu sometimes travel in large groups, and these groups can create thunder and lightning storms by working together.

Pikachu can use its electricity to roast berries. They're delicious!

Ash's Pikachu is a brave Pokémon that never lets its small size slow it down. It is cheerful and very loyal to its best buddy Ash, and it's friendly to most people and Pokémon it meets. It loves to battle and can become quite upset if kept out of the arena for too long!

Sometimes, Pikachu can get overloaded with electricity, and that can lead to a bad temper. When overloaded, its mood turns into electric sparks and storms. Pikachu doesn't mean to hurt anyone, of course—but watch out!

PIKA-CHOOSE WISELY!

Electric-type moves are super effective against what two types?
A) Steel and Bug
B) Water and Flying
C) Grass and Psychic

Answer: B) Water and Flying

PIKACHU'S KEY MOVES

Most of Pikachu's moves are Electric-type attacks, loaded with bright sparks and furious energy.

IRON TAIL: This one isn't an Electric-type move but a Steel-type attack. Pikachu learned this move in one of its most famous battles, against Rustboro Gym Leader Roxanne. Iron Tail is a great choice for Pikachu when it's fighting Ground-type Pokémon or others with resistance to its Electric-type attacks.

ELECTRO BALL: Ash's Pikachu learned this move not long after arriving in Unova, and it has been a favorite ever since. Pikachu's whole body becomes surrounded by a yellow glow, and it generates sparks that collect in its tail. When the Electro Ball is fully charged—WHAM!—Pikachu throws the crackling ball off its tail with a flip.

QUICK ATTACK: Sometimes a giant Thunderbolt is more power than Pikachu needs—and besides, Pikachu is known for its speed. Quick Attack lets it get in the first strike lightning-fast!

THUNDER: Pikachu learned Thunder during an early showdown in Dark City, though it no longer uses this move. It's a very powerful attack that can paralyze an opposing Pokémon. Thunder can really rattle an opponent, and Pikachu knows how to use it best!

THUNDERBOLT: This was Pikachu's go-to move during its travels in Kanto, but its aim wasn't always very good—it once hit some kids on a rooftop by accident! Pikachu has other powerful moves now, but Thunderbolt is always a reliable choice.

VOLT TACKLE: Only Pichu, Pikachu, and Raichu can use this rare, signature move—no other Pokémon are known to have mastered it. Ash's Pikachu learned Volt Tackle in a battle with Team Rocket, but doesn't use it anymore. It's a very powerful move, but it does cause recoil damage—sometimes enough to knock out the Pokémon using it!

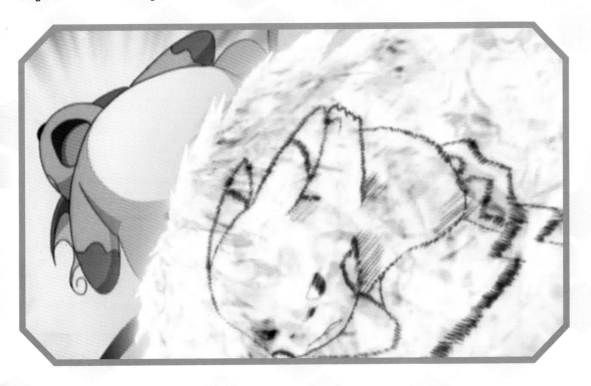

In addition to its moves, Pikachu also has the special Ability called Static! Whenever Pikachu takes a hit in battle, there's a chance that its opponent will be frozen in place and unable to move, as if it had grabbed a live wire.

YOU SAY YOU WANT AN EVOLUTION

All right—let's take a look at Pikachu's Evolutions, both what it evolves from and what it can evolve into!

PICHU

TYPE: Electric
CATEGORY: Tiny Mouse Pokémon
HEIGHT: 1'00"
WEIGHT: 4.4 lbs.

Pikachu evolve from Pichu, which have smaller electric pouches in their pink cheeks and don't have as much control over the electricity they store!

RAICHU

TYPE: Electric
CATEGORY: Mouse Pokémon
HEIGHT: 2'07"
WEIGHT: 66.1 lbs.

When Pikachu evolve, they evolve into Raichu, which are more aggressive and pack a much bigger electric punch than Pikachu—up to 100,000-volt bursts!

FOREVER PIKACHU!

Ash's Pikachu has had the opportunity to evolve more than once, but each time, it has chosen to keep its current state. Though this keeps it from learning certain moves like Hyper Beam, Ash's Pikachu is very happy with its decision.

Ash's Pikachu isn't the only Pikachu in the Pokémon world, though it's the most important one to Ash, of course! During their adventures, they have encountered other Trainers with Pikachu and even lots of Pikachu in the wild!

Where else besides battling for Ash could you find Pikachu? You're about to find out!

SURF'S UP, PIKACHU!

While visiting the Seafoam Islands in the Kanto region, Ash and Pikachu meet a surfer named Victor, who has a Pikachu of his own, called Puka. They quickly learn that Puka is a very unusual Pikachu—it has blue eyes, and it really understands the motion of the waves.

Thanks to Puka's special talent, Victor and his Pikachu have conquered every surfing challenge except one: a massive wave called Humunga-Dunga, which sweeps through the islands every twenty years. In fact, Victor tried to take it on twenty years ago, and failed...but that was before he met Puka!

This time, when the giant wave approaches, Puka is ready. Humunga-Dunga starts rolling in, and with the help of his amazing Pikachu, Victor successfully rides the biggest wave of his life, as Ash and his friends watch and cheer from the shore!

SPARKY

The friendship between Pikachu and Ash is mirrored in the friendship of another Pikachu named Sparky and its Trainer, Richie. Ash and Richie are both competing in the Indigo League when Team Rocket pulls off a scam and gets away with hundreds of Poké Balls, as well as Ash's Pikachu and Richie's Sparky!

After the friends are reunited, the League battle must go on—and it's Ash vs. Richie! Everyone's waiting in the stadium, but Ash is a no-show! As Team Rocket deliberately delays Ash's battle with Richie (because Ash won't give them Pikachu), the referee is about to disqualify Ash, but Richie asks for more time. He is sure his new friend will show.

When Ash gets there, Pikachu and his other Pokémon are wiped out from battling Team Rocket, and Richie wins easily. Ash questions his own abilities as a Trainer, but Richie talks sense into him. Later, Sparky and Pikachu combine forces to send Team Rocket blasting off!

POKÉMON YOU CAN COUNT ON
Sparky is Richie's heavy hitter, taking clean-up position in battle and against Team Rocket. Those Pikachu sure pack a powerful punch!

How do you know it's Sparky? It has a tuft of fur on its forehead!

SPARKY'S MOVES

- **AGILITY**
- **THUNDERBOLT**
- **THUNDERSHOCK**
- **THUNDER**

SAYING GOOD-BYE TO PIKACHU?

Ash would never leave Pikachu...or would he? The true test of friendship often involves saying goodbye at some point, and if it's meant to last forever, the friend will come back to you. Ash proved this while exploring a forest full of wild Pikachu.

After seeing a group of wild Pikachu, Ash thought it might be best for Pikachu to be with its own kind, but Pikachu knew in its heart that it belonged with Ash and quickly ran into Ash's arms. Right then they knew they'd be friends until the end.

While many Pikachu exist in the world of Pokémon, Ash's Pikachu is truly one of a kind. Always there when Ash needs it, ready to fight for any Pokémon in trouble with Team Rocket or anyone else who would try to capture or hurt them, Pikachu is a friend indeed.

Ash can always count on Pikachu through thick and thin, and that's why many Pokémon fans still come back to Pikachu as their favorite Pokémon year after year. Pikachu, we choose you!